JUST THE RIGHT CAKE

by CHRISTINA TOSI of MILK BAR®

illustrated by EMILY BALSLEY

Rocky Pond Books

It was a rainy day.
"A perfect day to bake a cake,"
thought Phil.

But if it had been a sunny day, Phil
would've thought the same thing.
Every day was a perfect day to
bake a cake if you asked him.

Especially when you baked with other people. Phil loved baking with his mom and dad. Today, though, he was baking with just his mom for the first time.

They made the same cake as always: double chocolate, his favorite!

But something was missing.

That weekend Phil went to his dad's new apartment.

LET'S BAKE A CAKE!

The kitchen was different but the recipe was the same:
double chocolate.

Dad liked it, but to Phil it didn't taste quite right.

It wasn't the frosting.

Phil wasn't sure.
He just knew the cake
wasn't the same.

The next day Phil made peanut butter
cookies with his friend Sammi.
Peanut butter was Phil's number one best snack!
He told Sammi about the two cakes that hadn't
tasted quite right.

Sammi told Phil that she thinks
every cake has a story.
And sometimes stories change.
Maybe Phil had a *new* story to tell.

Phil rode his bike and thought about what Sammi had said.
His life with his parents was different now, so maybe his *story*
was different too.

Phil decided to try
something new.
He asked his mom what
dessert *she* loved.
"Gooey chocolate brownies!"
she said.

They were perfect.

The next time Phil saw his dad they made a campfire in the backyard. Phil and Dad toasted marshmallows and made s'mores. Dad said they were his favorite, and Phil could see why.

They were delicious!

But something still didn't feel quite right.
The brownies were yummy and the s'mores
were great too.
But what was *Phil's* dessert?
What cake would tell *his* story?

The next day Phil went to the grocery store with his mom, and all of a sudden his imagination lit up. There were so many ingredients to choose from!

When Phil got home, he rushed into the kitchen to make his new cake.
The three layers were gooey chocolate brownie cake that his *mom* would love!

Between the layers Phil spread graham
crackers and gooey marshmallow cream
like the s'mores his *dad* loved.
Then Phil added the last touch.

This wasn't double chocolate frosting.
It was something new.
Peanut butter frosting!
Inspired by his favorite snack!

Phil stepped back and
looked at what
he'd made.

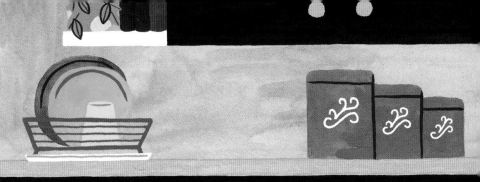

**A Chocolate Brownie
PB S'mores layer cake!**
He knew he had never tasted
anything like this before. It
was new and different,
but different could be great.

New could be exciting and special.

An adventure!

Phil was ready to see where his story would take him next.

PHIL'S CHOCOLATE BROWNIE PB S'MORES LAYER CAKE RECIPE

1 stick unsalted butter

½ cup chocolate chips

1 cup sugar

3 egg yolks

1 ½ tsp vanilla extract

⅓ cup flour

¼ cup cocoa powder

½ tsp salt

3 egg whites whipped until big and fluffy

1. Heat the oven to 325°F and pan spray three cake rounds.

2. In a large microwave safe bowl, melt the butter and chocolate chips together in 30-second spurts until smooth and combined.

3. Stir in sugar. Then egg yolks and vanilla. Then the flour, cocoa powder, and salt, mixing until smooth and combined.

4. Whisk in the fluffy egg whites until smooth and combined.

5. Pour the brownie cake batter evenly across the greased pans and bake at 325°F for 20 minutes.

6. Cool completely at room temperature before removing from the pans.

7. On a platter, layer each brownie cake round with marshmallow creme, graham cracker crumbs, and peanut butter frosting.
(Grown-ups: Don't forget to torch the top!)

marshmallow creme

graham crackers

peanut butter frosting

To my wonderful mother, wonderful father, and wonderful stepparents.

Thank you for a lifetime of late-night grocery store runs and for cheering me on in my baking journey. —C.T.

To my mom—thank you for sharing your love of art with me. Your encouragement and support has inspired me in so many ways! —E.B.

ROCKY POND BOOKS
An imprint of Penguin Random House LLC, New York

First published in the United States of America by Rocky Pond Books, an imprint of Penguin Random House LLC, 2023

Text copyright © 2023 by Christina Tosi
Illustrations copyright © 2023 by Emily Balsley

Rocky Pond Books & colophon are trademarks of Penguin Random House LLC.
The Penguin colophon is a registered trademark of Penguin Books Limited.

Visit us online at penguinrandomhouse.com.

Library of Congress Cataloging-in-Publication Data is available.

Manufactured in China
ISBN 9780593110713
1 3 5 7 9 10 8 6 4 2
TOPL

Design by Jennifer Kelly • Text set in Avenir
The art for this book was created using gouache and ink, composited in Photoshop.